Enjoy

A ROMAN AFFAIR

Short Story to Red Fury Rage

R-Pride Publishing
www.jfridgley.com

JF RIDGLEY

Dedication to
Joe
My best friend

Chapter 1

Introductions

Julia Procilla Valeria

I cannot believe what happened. It started out perfectly. Then, he turned on me. How could he do this after all I had done for him?

I remember that fall day when I fell in love with Gaius Suetonius Paulinus. It was at Tullius Marcus's afternoon party in Rome. I have always loved parties, meeting people, gossiping, and laughing with my friends. Being barely fifteen at the time, my parents absolutely never had a problem getting me to attend any celebration.

Once at the party, my girlfriends and I would instantly melt into our small group to feast on whatever the latest gossip was, mostly learned that morning at the baths. Oh, we all could have stayed at home and been pampered in our private baths. But how could we when gossip was so much richer in the public thermae.

That particular afternoon, the gossip was overflowing with news about a new senator by the name of Gaius Suetonius Paulinus. We each were giddy to find out if what we had heard was true. And it was true.

We swooned the moment Suetonius appeared in the atrium of Tullius' townhouse. He was every bit of a lean, hard, tanned, twenty-five year old senator. Confidence pulsed from him as he greeted everyone. Like a tidal wave, we felt his presence from across the room.

An impudent nerve set off between all of us--who was to demand his complete attention? Attempting to maintain a proper appearance of propriety, composure, and friendship, our gazes still dripped with desire. Over our wine goblets, we observed his every move as carefully as any animal on the hunt, watching to see where his first glance fell. It was I who won.

We all pretended as if we had seen absolutely nothing, that his intrusion into our midst was purely an invasion. Somehow, I managed to feign indifference as he worked his way toward us. It was difficult to not act as a victor and remain indifferent as if he did not exist. I pretended to be stunned when he joined us, but I most certainly rewarded him with my most apt attention.

My friends—or should I say competitors—each continued to gush with suggestions of what tray of food seemed extra tasty. Asked ever important questions of his appointment. Or asked him his thoughts on any upcoming legal cases he may have to deal with. Each hoping I would ultimately lose, of course.

Claiming a goblet of wine, Suetonius stood there enduring my friends' efforts to be charming, nodding his ever-so-handsome face. His sandalwood and cedar fragrance instantly floated over me, shutting off any conversation I may have espoused. In other words, I was speechless.

As a perfect patrician, he respectfully responded to each plea for his attention, only to have my friends drown in his gleaming brown gaze. I smiled appropriately and resumed my interest in their vain attempts to lure him away. He accepted their benign interests with a tilt of his sensuous lips. It seemed so natural to him since command seemed to draw to him as panther to its prey—me.

I remember the thrill of my hand brushing the vibrant green pallium draped over his broad shoulder and entrapped by a modest gold link belt that surrounded his narrow waist. As he talked, I could not help but notice his arms corded from hours at the gymnasium and training with the legion. A slow ache itched over me to feel them draw me close to his body.

Once Suetonius had endured my friends' endless chatter, he turned to me, asking if I would show him about Tullius' elaborate gardens. I pretended to be stunned that he would consider that I would be knowledgeable about such things. Of course, I modestly accepted and left the small group now dripping with absolute envy.

That was not the last garden we visited. Oh no. We deliberately found each other at the theater, games, the horse races, or simply wandered the markets together. We found any reason to slip away to anywhere to be alone, to talk, stroll, and listen to one another.

I will never forget the day I was supposed to be shopping for Saturnalia when I met Suetonius in Gardens of Sallust blustering with dry autumn leaves. It was here that Suetonius claimed my first kiss. My heart melted into his palms.

Gaius Suetonius Paulinus

I cannot believe what happened. It started out perfectly, then she turned on me. How could she do this after all I had done for her?

To this day, I have loved Procilla. She was all I saw the day we met at Tullius Marcus's party which was nothing more than an ordinary gathering. I came to celebrate and announce my appointment as a *junior praetor.* I had come to begin to glean my own influence among Tullius' senatorial guests.

The moment I saw Procilla, I knew I must have her. I endured her friends' attempts to distract my attention with their prattle. She, too, endured those same attempts, standing beside me like a goddess—the most beautiful girl ever seen in Rome. It was her glowing face, the silk of her mahogany hair arranged in ringlets over her shoulder, her brown eyes bright and laughing. She was so free and alive. Radiant.

The brush of her hand against my side sent shock waves through me. Instantly, I had to have Procilla alone, to myself. Having consumed enough prattle I asked her if she would show me the gardens. Her gaze instantly ignited like a stary night as she graciously agreed.

Strolling the gardens was the last thing I wanted, but I relished that Procilla was there beside me, properly smiling to any who passed us. Against my desire, we modestly kept a proper distance. Even so, she seemed to cling to my every word—words I know not where they came from. But I stood taller that day.

During our many escapes from Rome's entertainments, I learned quickly that her radiance could darken like a storm cloud when concern greeted her. It may be nothing more than disloyalty, a concern for her family, or if there was a threat to Rome. If more citizens had Procilla's sincerity and loyalty, Rome would glow as she did.

From that day at Tullius Marcus's party Procilla became my life. Until that very moment, I only lived to care for her. I lived to see her daily. I begged to hear her laugh. I basked in her sweet perfume of jasmine, which was to become the cloud she walked in. Then, I knew there would never be enough jewels in the world for her. I wanted to give them all to her and then remove them ever so slowly. It was then that I wanted Procilla as mine. Only mine. But now....

CHAPTER 2

DISAPPOINTMENTS

Suetonius

I was beyond incensed, when Procilla's father chose to marry her to a filthy, provincial equestrian. This family of Gnaeus Julius Agricola quickly rose to senatorial rank by kissing every butt in Rome. However, I hated the man simply because he had claimed what was already mine. Procilla. My own father was impressed that I had even attracted Procilla's attentions and quickly had proceeded to make the proper offers to join our houses in marriage. Our hopes dangled on a thin thread.

Procilla was from an esteemed senatorial family-well established in Rome. Mine had crawled up through the ranks of a common equestrian. And now I, unproven and young, had been barely clinging to any hope of becoming a senator. Now that I had begun to successfully make that climb, I wanted Procilla at my side.

The day my father received Procillius Valerius's refusal of marriage, I destroyed everything of value in my father's house. And my father paid no mind to my fury.

Procilla

Usually, my visits with Suetonius were with the belief that I was simply attending Rome's entertainments with my friends or just shopping. But, when Father learned the truth of what I was doing, he became terribly upset.

I remember the day Suetonius's father approached my father with a request to join our houses in marriage. My father was his usual gracious self, pretending interest, hearing the man's offer, listening to his reasoning, and then claiming to consider the arrangement.

The instant Suetonius' father left, Father set his goblet down harshly on the serving table, turned to me, and emphatically said, "No. Not with that house."

I was then sent immediately to our family villa in Cemenelum to recover my sanity. My personal slave was removed to the kitchens for her lack of attention. A new, more attentive slave was found, one not so easily seduced by Suetonius' compliments and gifts.

Suetonius and my letters became tear stained with our broken hearts. Our only consolation was my brother, Valerius, who transported our love letters.

Over these last few months, Valerius and Suetonius had become fast friends. They both loved Rome and all it stood for. Valerius had gleaned his appointment with the legions, while Suetonius had pursued his place in the Senate. Unlike Suetonius, my brother was better suited among military since he had no polish for politics. Yet, even as my brother pleaded with Father to reconsider the marriage arrangements, Father simply refused to listen.

I begged Mother and Father to reconsider Suetonius. Yet again, they ignored my pleas. Suetonius was nothing to them, yet he was my everything, even my life. How could I give my heart to anyone but Suetonius?

My parents must have talked the matter through and determined that, since I was so easily infatuated, it was time to consider another marriage arrangement.

Soon thereafter, I learned that Father had found an acceptable arrangement with the senatorial house of 'Gnaeus Julius Luci filius Anansi's Agricola Foro Julii.' I simply refused to comply. However, the arrangements were made without any of my input. I was simply a prop for this proceeding, much as the flowers were.

The fateful wedding day arrived, and I met my future husband. I was determined to remain faithful to Suetonius no matter—that is until I met Gnaeus Julius Agricola.

I believe it was the gentleness of Gnaeus' gaze and his eloquent poise, that I soon learned, he had to be the kindest man in all of Rome and the most elegant senator. My resistance simply melted like sun-warmed butter the instant he stood next to me in his senatorial toga, blazing white with its wide purple hem. My hand still thrills with that memory of him sliding the wedding band around my heart.

Gnaeus and I were immediately happy. We stayed at his parent's villa in Massilia for as long as possible until he had to return to Rome for the business of being a senator.

I soon admired him almost as a god. It was obvious Gnaeus genuinely cared for the people of Rome—plebeian or patrician.

Shall I say, he melted my heart and won all my attentions. And soon I carried his son.

It was in April when Gnaeus and I attended a spring party that Suetonius and his new wife Maria were in attendance. Our host announced to all present that the gods had granted Gnaeus and I a new citizen for Rome. Cheers rose to the rafters. Yet, the instant Suetonius learned I carried Gnaeus' child; his gaze became vehement.

Suetonius had arrived with his new wife, Maria Crassa. Not only had I learned at the thermae about their marriage, but I also overheard that Suetonius had proceeded to gain the favor of the Emperor Caligula. And because of that, his father's house had joined with the family of Crassus. I knew that the marriage was not for love. Nor would it ever be so.

It was well-known that Maria was unconcerned for any pleasures of Rome, preferring to run her country villa instead. She was not elegant, and obviously was not enraptured with the social engagements demanded of senators. This was something I knew Suetonius relished. And, over the years, her womb was never blessed with a child, not due to infertility. It was due to the lack of any intention to fill it.

June 13th, the gods blessed us with a boy, and Gnaeus and I were beyond joy. Our son, who also bore the honored name of his father—Gnaeus Julius Agricola, was healthy, strong, and beyond beautiful. We enjoyed each breath Julius claimed, and was enthralled by every step the boy took. Soon, Julius adored his father as much as I did. There was no happier family in all of Rome.

Chapter 3

Realities

Suetonius

Procilla carried his child? That bastard had claimed that which was mine. That fact burned like a rash by simply knowing that Gnaeus was enjoying the only love of my life. It was obvious, now, that Procilla adored her new husband. They even appeared perfect together, which only made my marriage all the more sickening. If that were possible.

My wife, Maria Crassa, niece of Marcus Crassus had the wealth to see to my appointment into the Senate and eventually consul to Mauritania. Fortunately for me, she shared no affection for Rome but only for her father's villa—granted to us as a wedding gift. While Maria attended her villa outside the city, I resided in my townhouse in Rome. A very compatible arrangement.

My time at the Imperial palace was challenging to say the least. Caligula was precarious. But our illustrious emperor seemed to take a liking to my advice. Before Caligula appointed me as consul to Mauretania, I overheard him fuming over Gnaeus' refusal to prosecute a fellow senator – Albinius Crator. I, too, disliked this fool who had once attempted to dishonor my family's name. Thus providing the perfect revenge which was mine to claim.

I was straightforward in convincing Caligula to reconsider punishing Gnaeus for his arrogance in challenging the imperial opinions. How dare the Senate or this senator, in any way, refuse the emperor's judgments!

By the time I had arrived as consul in Mauretania, I learned that Gnaeus had been immediately executed for his actions. Even if I had influenced Caligula's thoughts, I carried no guilt in the matter. However, I made certain that Procilla never knew what I had orchestrated on my behalf.

Procilla

My Beloved Procilla
Take care of our son.
I will eternally send you my love.
Gnaeus

How many times had I read Gnaeus' last words? I am beyond memorizing such simple words. As I read his letter to me and our son, I heard his beloved voice and felt him near.

The letter arrived with the horrid news that Caligula had ordered my husband executed without any compassion, without any chance for me to hold him in my arms again. Without him ever holding his son again. Or saying goodbye, except through a brief message written within seconds of losing his life. My good and gentle husband whom I loved with my entire existence was gone.

How could Caligula destroy our lives like this for no other reason than to show his power. To display the consequences of challenging his imperial decrees.

I lost everything I valued but our son, who had lost his beloved father whom he adored. Julius constantly asked, "When is papa coming home? When, Mama?"

My answer was excruciating. "Soon, Julius. Soon." How horrible is it to lie to one so young?

I hated existing in Rome. How could I endure a cruel city without Gnaeus? I was beyond devastation. I wanted nothing more than to join Gnaeus but, how could I? I had our son to consider. The child carried his father's name as well as his family's ancestorial name. It became as my responsibility to see that Julius respected and honored what his father had left him.

Like Gnaeus' family, our lives dissolved into horror. Gnaeus' father retired from the Senate to return to Massilia. They welcomed me to join them. However, after Gnaeus' funeral, Julius and I returned to my parent's villa in Cemenelum, wanting never to see Rome again.

Years before, my father Procillius Valerius had passed on to the afterlife. So, my mother and my life now rested in my brother's hands. Valerius held no interest in the family villa, but he saw that my little family had the funds to survive. I had my son; Valerius had his legions. I allowed my life to revolve around my son's welfare and nothing more. Julius became my life.

To my surprise, after Julius and I returned to my family's villa, Suetonius' first letter arrived. He sounded terribly upset that Caligula had acted in such manner to execute Gnaeus over *such a stupid reason. He said it was a very wrong decision, and that alone was the reason enough for the Senate to welcome the execution of the emperor, which had occurred shortly after Gnaeus' execution. Suetonius wished me much happiness with my son and asked if he could visit upon his return.*

Of course, I said yes.

CHAPTER 4

CHALLENGES

Suetonius

Her door slave, Milo, kept me informed about Procilla while I was with the legions. I wrote her. I sent her gifts by the galley full. I memorized her letters of gratitude and endured her prideful dialogue on the growing boy.

After my return to Rome, I took every advantage to see Procilla. I wanted nothing more than to marry her. However, I was too far into debt with my rise with the Senate that I could not return Maria's dowry.

Yet, if Procilla would have considered such arrangement, I would have found a way. She had even refused her brother's suggestion that she consider our marriage. Procilla truly had devoted herself to her son who proceeded to grow up into the very image of his despicable father.

Over the next years, I was only to remain a close friend, willing to assist with any concern. I recommended the best teachers for her son. I explained the legions to Julius. I played wooden swords with the boy, and I even went so far as to teach him to ride. In an odd sense, Julius had become the son I had wanted to share with his mother.

Years swiftly passed with Rome's demands. However, when the time came, I persuaded Procilla to bring Julius to Rome to further his education there. I convinced her it was time that Julius experienced our great empire's wealth and pleasures. I had hoped her return to a social life would bring Procilla into my arms.

Procilla

Gnaeus took to Suetonius. That pleased me beyond measure. The boy deeply missed his father, and Suetonius seemed concerned for Julius. Over the next years, Suetonius saw to whatever my mother and I needed. He also stepped in when Julius needed guidance and advice. It was glorious watching Julius grow up under Suetonius' attentions.

However, my heart broke when I envisioned Gnaeus teaching his son such things as riding horses, hunting, and Julius listening to his father's stories of the legions instead of Suetonius'.

Even as our affections rekindled into a remarkably close friendship, I refused his wishes to join our families in marriage. I had my son's reputation and future to think about, so nothing transpired between us other than friendship.

Suetonius struggled with this. In time, he convinced me to return to Rome. It was a pleasant distraction from the past as my son experienced the marvel of our city under his guidance.

Julius seemed to come to life. He begged to go to the Circus Maximus and the gladiatorial matches. He cheered for Suetonius's Reds. He delighted in the puppet shows on the streets and even a few of the theaters' plays. He discovered friends of other senators' sons and went to the gymnasium constantly.

I was, once again, enjoying parties, the daily gossip, and the latest fashions that Suetonius indulged upon me. I began to thrive as my son had. It became impossible for me to return to my villa.

As sons do, the time had arrived when Julius was ready to continue his learning in Massilia. Gnaeus' father wanted Julius to go there for his rhetorical education as his father had. Suetonius agreed. He said it was a wise choice. To say I was lonely, would be to say the Tiber is wet.

Chapter 5

Conveniences

Procilla

One particular winter day became the worst of my days after Julius left. I had gone shopping simply to get out of the house before I slit my wrists. The instant Suetonius saw me in the Forum markets, concern exploded on his face as if I had grown horns. Immediately distressed, he determined that I must smile.

He fawned over me worse than any mother, buying me this or that, pointing out insidious behaviors of passers-byes to make me laugh. There seemed to be a constant flow of such entertainment.

We were once again in the Garden of Sallust, when I finally admitted I missed Julius more than I dreamed possible. I could not bear the thought that my little boy was becoming a young man and would soon be leaving for the legions, which was Julius' ultimate dream.

As the sun set, Suetonius invited me for dinner, promising that he would belay any further misery that certainly awaited me at my townhouse. Which was true. Those hours there, without Julius, had become unbearable. I claimed his invitation almost without hesitation.

I could not believe how horrendously plain Suetonius' townhouse was or how pathetically he had been living. His house on the Pincius hill bore outdated paintings, no curtains, and was barely filled with the necessary furniture.

He never stopped apologizing, assuring me that Maria cared more about the manure for her vineyards than his town-house. I believed him.

I suggested a few things to do to enliven the space, and he proceeded to ask me to oversee any decorations I felt suitable. As the walls came to life, so did I—or shall I say, we came to life.

Suetonius

Our affair began when Milo's man assigned to follow Procilla informed me that she had gone shopping and was apparently saddened from the absence of her son.

When I found her in the Forum markets, the brilliance was void in her face. She was wearing a plain blue stola and palla. Her hair was arranged in a style my wife would have preferred—a plain and simple bun. This was so unlike her. She normally put elegance to shame.

Therefore, I determined that I had to return the gleam to her lifeless eyes. As we strolled in a garden as we once had years before, she finally admitted. "I truly miss my son." It was said with so much pain that I believed her.

"Then come. Join me for dinner," I pleaded.

Surprisingly, she agreed.

I sent my personal slave ahead of us to make sure the slaves attended us as though we were imperial. The evening became what I had once dreamed of before her father refused my marriage proposal.

The air was calm, pleasant. We talked of nothing and taunted each other over everything. I saw that her goblet flowed endlessly with the best wine Rome could offer. I held her as she shed tears regarding her son's absence that fed into how she longed for her husband's touch. Such words sickened me, but I feigned sympathy. Finally, I heard her laugh over something I thought was ridiculous.

Soon, we were feasting on starved flesh. My dreams and fantasies were satiated. I watched as life returned to her soul, fed only by my attentions. To my delight, many nights followed.

Gossip got back to Maria. This was the first sign of jealousy I had ever witnessed from my wife. I had actually forgotten that I was married to that woman. I thought I had become invisible to her.

In a vicious letter, Maria threatened to reveal our affair to her father. In retaliation, I informed Maria that if is she said anything to anyone, I would see that she and her villa would be totally destroyed. Nothing more was shared on this matter.

CHAPTER 6

IMAGININGS

Suetonius

My townhouse blossomed with Procilla's touch. I could have cared less if the walls were painted totally brown. If she were to wish that color, I would have relished in it. Our love nest became as elegant as she was.

Fortunate for me, Procilla and I kept our time together without Rome's notice. We attended parties separately. Mingled separately. Departed separately. Only sharing the evenings as lovers. We were determined to be seen as simply friends while enjoying this challenge before the gossiping eyes and sharp tongues discovered the truth.

After Julius completed his education in Massilia and returned to Rome, we were obligated to be even more cautious. Fortunately, he was consumed with the desire to follow in his father's footsteps. I considered seeing that he did. Obviously, my affections for the boy were still alive and well.

Little do I believe Procilla realized that my dreams with her had claimed my life in every way. I would have conquered the world for her … then.

In AD 60, Nero assigned me to Britannia as consul, which could have been devastating for me but ultimately was not. My vast friend and ally, Valerius was to go with me as my first centurion to the XIVth Legio - Gemina.

Procilla begged me to arrange for Julius to accompany us for his first appointment with the legions as tribune. With me and her brother in Britannia and Julius ready for his first appointment to the legions, how could I refuse?

Procilla

Shortly after Julius' betrothal to Domitia, her father and I focused all of our attentions on planning for Julius to enter the Senate. He needed a tour of duty with the legions to begin. Since Suetonius was appointed to Britannia as consul and my brother appointed as his first centurion, I begged Suetonius to get Julius an appointment with them. At least my boy had watchful eyes on him.

But not watchful enough. I never dreamed that Julius could embarrass me with this idiocy by getting a Britanni slave girl pregnant with a son. Suetonius and I agreed that we must deter his blind stupidity for this girl.

I suggested that I bring Domitia, his betrothed, to Britannia to get them married, in hopes of reminding Julius why he was there. My brother and Suetonius made the arrangements to make this happen.

Of course, Domitia was excited for such an adventure to be wed to the man of her dreams. However, it failed to turn out that way.

CHAPTER 7

REALITIES

Suetonius

Julius was an absolute asset with the legions. But he was stupid enough to get involved with the Iceni queen's daughter. Procilla was beside herself with fear of humiliation. She asked if she could bring his betrothed to Britannia and get the boy married to a proper Roman girl. Valerius and I agreed to assist in this unusual celebration. It was a total failure.

Julius proved his worth to me as my second-in-command during Boudica's revolt. The boy obviously had the talents that Rome needed. I, proudly, could easily see him standing beside me on the floor of the Senate one day.

Then the fool wanted to bring the Britanni bitch and her whelp back to Rome as his wife and son, something which Rome would never recognize as a lawful union. Not only would this mean a humiliating divorce from the house of Decidianus, but a horror to Procilla.

Procilla was obessed that this had to be stopped in any way possible. She wanted nothing to do with this embarrassment to her family's name as well as her damned husband's name.. She insisted that we do anything to prevent Julius from bringing those filthy barbarians back to Rome.

Once I managed to see that the Britanni revolt destroyed, I arranged to see that Julius was recalled back to Rome as swiftly as possible. I refused Julius' ire by refusing his request to use a cohort of scouts to find the kidnapped girl and her little bastard. I reminded Julius that he was of more value to Rome, and that he was wedded to a proper Roman girl who would be an honor to his family's name and to him. He ignored me entirely.

The task of seeing to his nephew's return became his uncle's obsession. To say Valerius was livid would be an understatement. The very idea of his nephew taking that whore and whelp back to Rome ignited his centurion temper. "Over my dead body, he will."

Procilla's brother never shared how nor what he contrived to prevent his nephew from taking *his little family* back to Rome; but *his little family* ultimately did not return with him. Julius, however, did return to Rome totally against his will.

Procilla

After Julius was forced home from Britannia, the relationships between us became very strained to say the least. In his blind rage, Julius blamed us all for ruining his life. I believed surely, once he returned home to his new family, he would regain his senses. However, he did not.

Never could I understand how Julius could embarrass me in this way. After all that we had done for him. He well knew that his desires went against Roman law, and still he was willing to toss away all the opportunities Rome offered him.

Suetonius had even written a letter that had arranged for an early appointment into the Senate, for which I was extremely grateful. However, Julius even rejected that opportunity over that Britanni bitch and her whelp.

Julius continued to reveal that he had little or no respect for anyone or his family's reputation. This inconsideration completely devastated Suetonius and my time together, making our encounters contentious. Suetonius groused about how Julius knew better and that his talents were being wasted. I fumed over the potential gossip and humiliation he was bringing to our houses, not to speak of the heartbreak to Domitia. Thus, I returned to my villa to escape.

CHAPTER 8

SURPRISES

Suetonius

Should I say I was shocked to learn of Julius' actions after he returned to home. I actually thought that Julius would finally forget that bitch and her whelp and settle down, but he did not.

Julius, however, never gave up on his insidious dream of returning to Britannia to find his whelp. When positions in Britannia opened for tribunes, Julius nearly got his wish to return. Britannia's new consul desperately wanted him. After all, Julius knew the land, the people, and had the experience with the legions already there.

Once again, Procilla begged me to find any another assignment for her son. "Anywhere but to Britannia. Please, Suetonius." It truly made sense to me. It would be more advisable for Julius to go elsewhere.

Salvius Otho Titianus needed a quaestor with him in Asia and was willing to ask for Julius' appointment. It offered the next step in her son's career, so I suggested it to Titianus. He considered the idea, and it was accomplished.

My only gain in this appointment left me thinking I would owe Titianus some favor. But upon Titianus' return from Asia, the senator assured me I did not owe him a damn thing. Julius had been exceptional.

However, whatever respect Julius had for me was totally destroyed. I was blamed for ruining any attempt for him to return to Britannia and had managed to send him to Ephesus. However true that may be, his mother remained innocent.

Not only was I not pleased about Julius' contempt, but I was also even less pleased with the direction our empire was going. Anyone who cared a whit over the Empire's future was concerned. Soon after Julius returned to Rome, our glorious city burned to the ground, the treasury was emptied, and the unpaid legions had taken the throne as theirs to appoint the next Caesar.

Yet, what stunned me the most was Procilla. She was far more obsessed about her son returning to Britannia and her embarrassing position in society than the welfare of Rome. It was all she rattled on about when we were together.

Procilla

When Julius came up for another appointment with the legions, I begged Suetonius to get him an appointment to anywhere but Britannia. And Juno be praised, Julius was appointed quaestor to Titianus and fortunately, to the other side of the Empire. Ephesus.

When Julius did return, to his surprise, he did so to a beautiful little girl, Julia. It pleased me that he found much pride and joy in having a daughter.

However, I was continuously bothered by ridiculous rumors that stirred around Rome that Domitia had had an affair and that the baby girl belonged to whoever the lover was. Utterly impossible! Domitia would never do such a thing!

Regardless of what Suetonius thinks or any of those wagging tongues, I know Domitia would never dishonor my son's house nor her father's house with a so-called affair. She had been raised better than to endure such malignancy.

CHAPTER 9

MUTINY

Suetonius

One can never forget the day when the legions went mad with power. It changed the course of the Empire completely because the legions assumed, since they fought and died for Rome, that they were a better judge of an emperor than the gods. First, Rome lost the Republic and now it had lost the gods' favor.

Like the rest of Rome, I, also, had lost what existed of my life. Procilla, now, spent her time at her villa with her bastard granddaughter while I remained trapped in Rome attempting to stop the destruction of our glorius empire.

And, when Julius did return from Asia, he bore an even greater vile mindset toward me — as if I were totally responsible for all of his appointments. For Procilla's sake, I kept silent to these facts. Her son would never believe the truth from me anyway.

Nero was the first fool. He believed the people would delight in his *New Rome*. Due to his astronomical taxes and the late pay to the legions, even I voted to title Nero 'enemy of the state" which led to his suicide. I would have changed that vote had I known what was to come.

First, the western legions favored Galba, an old bald, fool who was lost in the past when rulers ruled the lives of his men. As I expected, Julius served Galba quite well.

I was impressed with Julius' valor, until Galba ordered him to collect the temple goods that Nero had auctioned off to pay for his golden creation. What was more, Maria had filled her villa with them.

I had to endure Julius' delight in reclaiming each and every auctioned object, granting Maria no quarter of respect. I was incensed when he even raped my townhouse of my temple goods. After all I had done for this ungrateful little prick, he could not ignore even one of our favorites.

I did not think matters could go worse. But they did. Not only was my beloved empire was crumbling, but I had to endure my pathetic wife continually mourning her lost treasures. Then, after all these years that I had devoted to Procilla and her son, they both ignored me like I was no more than a filthy slave.

Ultimately, Milo informed me that Procilla, whom I had seen that she got her wants and desires for her and her wretched son, was seeing Menius Plautius, a common, filthy, abhorrent equestrian.

Procilla

No one knew what the gods were doing, or if they were doing, or if they cared that Rome was being torn apart by a continuous procession of emperors.

Because of this, I had begun to find Suetonius more disturbing than usual. He continually ranted on about politics, legion loyalty, and the actions in Rome. When he started on Julius reclaiming Maria's temple goods, I could not bear it any longer.

Menius Plautius had entered my life then. We had met while Suetonius and Maria were dealing with Julius over the temple goods.

Menius is, at least, pleasant to be with, and is not interested in the depleted treasury, nor who the legions were appointing as the next emperor. I discovered he was a delightful man lost in his passion toward delivering his merchant goods. In fact, that is how we met.

Menius was dealing with his cloth merchant when I entered the fabric store. I had found a bolt of fabric I liked. Our gazes connected. Smiles were shared. Moments later, the store owner gifted me with the entire bolt of fabric…'as a gift from an admirer.' Menius was gone before I could properly thank him.

Then we attended a party the following week. I was wearing my new stola made from his 'gift'. He joined me, complimenting on the fabric. "Yes, a gift from an admirer," I informed him.

Menius' grin drew a long-forgotten blush to my cheeks as we began a conversation regarding who this 'admirer' may be. Unlike Suetonius, who wore a battle hard body, Menius was as fluffy and comfortable as a pillowed lounger and was doubly delightful.

After many occasions together, he invited me to a play at the Marcellus Theater, and afterward, we were strolling in the gardens. I remember, now, that it was cloudy and threatening rain. Rather chilly, so I had tightened my palla about me. I could tell that Menius was fretting over some issue, carrying it like a heavy parcel. It made the afternoon as bleak as the tragedy performed earlier. Alas, I got him to tell me what was bothering him. He stopped his thick set frame and clasped my hands.

My palla fluttered away with my soul when Menius informed me that he had overheard gossip that my dead husband had been maligned and thus executed by someone who had twisted Caligula's thoughts against Gnaeus.

"No. No. Who would do such a thing? Who?"

Menius frowned, his gaze offered a suggestion before he spoke, "Someone who wanted you in their life instead of Gnaeus?"

I could not stop shaking my head. That person could only be Suetonius. No. Not after all he had done for me and Julius.

But, as the pictures and memories flickered through my brain, it all became a serious consideration. What if Menius was right? My shock turned to fury. "How do you know this?"

Menius drew me to a private bench to explain that he had recently purchased one of the imperial slaves. The slave had been present when Caligula had my husband executed.

Disbelief reigned. I had to talk to this slave myself. That was when Menius called the man forward from the shadows.

Torture was unnecessary. I knew all that the slave said, all he described, was true. Still, I refused to believe them. They had to be lying. They were only intent on destroying Suetonius.

I went to my villa to escape the impossibilities, but all the memories, words, pictures followed me, joining with those that were already awaiting me in Cemenelum.

I was not certain about any of this until Suetonius burst into my villa with accusations about Menius. He stormed in, unannounced, uninvited, reminding me of all he had done for me, and accusing me of being unfaithful. In doing so, he began throwing vases, pillows, flipping triclinium loungers aside, destroying everything.

His fury failed to match mine! Suetonius had no place to accuse anyone of being unfaithful. Nor had he been the only one assisting the other.

Had I not made his townhome presentable to Rome? Had I not made certain that his reputation was well-received everywhere I went? Instead, he had lied to me. Something I had never done to him.

This fact nearly destroyed me. His demolition of my house stopped instantly when I coldly and calmly asked if he had contrived to get Caligula to execute Gnaeus.

Silent, he set the vase down on its table and looked at me. It was then I knew all that Menius and his slave had said was absolutely true.

My soul had been shredded with Domitia's rumors, but now my life disintegrated. I plucked the unbroken vase and threw it at him Until then, I had never known fear.

Suetonius charged, fists drawn, eyes blazing. He threw me on a lounger, his fist ready to pummel me. Clutching the cape pin I had given him, I lashed at him, cutting a deep gash in his cheek. Shock coated his face long enough to have my slaves remove him, cursing and screaming from me. I live only because the slaves

"I will see you dead for this. I will see your son as dead the as I did his father. Furthermore, I will see the house of Gnaeus Julius Agricola forever forgotten!"

Now, I have no choice but to do what I never dreamed possible. I must kill that which had brought me so much joy, *happiness, and wellbeing before he destroys my son. Suetonius must die.*

Suetonius

Used. Played. Wounded. Discarded like trash. That was what I felt the day I was thrown from Procilla's villa. Blinded by my fury, I found the nearest taverna and got drunk, something I never do in the presence of strangers. I drank to oblivion.

The following morning, returning to consciousness and sense, I calmly returned to Rome. By which time, I had drawn a plan to destroy Menius, Procilla, and the entire house of Gnaeus Julius Agricola once and for all.

I had no idea such an opportunity would be provided by our gluttonous emperor Vitellius. Again, I had become a major influence on this imbecilic idiot. It nearly worked.

Fini

ACKNOWLEDGMENTS

It takes a lot to bring a good story to the world—almost like giving birth. And I have so many to thank. Cathy Helms—Avalon Graphics.org—for a magnificent cover design She is amazing. Deb McKew and Charla White—Wordsaplenty.com—for their editing that helped this affair make sense. Lisa Despain—book2Bestseller.com—for her excellent eye for detail with formatting and helping me get this story published and noticed. And Heidi Draper—etsy.com/shop/EWDesignsStudio—for the custom creation of Procilla's cape pine. Patrick and Yvonne—Urated.com—for all your help with marketing and website designs.

Finally, to the many friends who patiently listened to me talk about my favorite topic…my stories. You all are the absolute best friends and remarkable professionals to ever work with. God bless you all.

And to you dear reader. You are so loved and appreciated beyond measure.

ABOUT THE AUTHOR

I love the ancient world. Even after years of researching and many trips to England and Italy of my stories, I am still fascinated by what I find for to bring to life in my novels. I love ancient world of Rome And, I love bringing this world to life in my award-winning stories of power, greed, violence, and love. It is never dull.

Be sure to stop by my website to discover more and to also sign up for my newsletter so you never miss what's coming next. For example, to enter the latest promotion to WIN a custom-made prize by Heidi. *Be assured that I do not share your address or send an excessive barrage of information.*

To sign up for my newsletter visit
http://www.jfridgley.com
I would love to hear from you so contact me at
jfridgley@jfridgley.com

For more about these books and short stories visit
https://www.jfridgley.com/historical-fiction/

Coming in 2022:

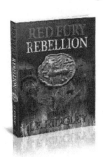

Book 2 of the Agricola series Red Fury

CHAPTER 1

Squawking seagulls circled in the blue sky as the Roman galley tugged for its freedom in the restless water of Porta Liguria pier. Slaves piled cargo boxes on the deck while sailors finished securing the galley to its moorings.

Standing on the deck, observing everything before him, Julius inhaled the familiar, rain-washed fragrances from the nearby Maritime mountains, the sea, and all that had once been his home. His face snarled with disgust.

Nearly two years ago, he had been ordered to Britannia and had been one of those polished tribunes parading on the pier among the citizens clustered in groups, waiting for someone to arrive or to weep their good-byes. That was when Rome held his heart and loyalty. No longer. Not after the Consul Suetonius refused his request to bring Rhianna and Gnaeus back with him.

His Uncle Valerius' threat over that issue still echoed in his brain, "You will do as ordered and return to Rome even if I have to send you back like a slave." Julius' wrists, raw from the slave manacles that had cut into his flesh and soul, had proved his uncle's words. This last month at sea had seemed endless after his uncle had knocked him unconscious, leaving him chained to the bunk inside the galley. Vomiting, dizziness, and pain had frothed in his skull for an eternity.

Each time the galley pulled into a port, his uncle's appointed guards had bolted his cabin door, confining him like an animal until the galley left the next day. Only when the shore was out of sight was he freed from his entrapment to walk the deck with the guards trailing him like dogs.

Britannia had become the land he loved with his heart and soul now. This was where Rhianna and his son lived— without him—because Rome had forced him to leave them.

Now, that same loyal Roman citizen standing there, looking at his past, was dead.

Lugh, his personal slave, had kept him from throwing every piece of his Roman life overboard, including himself. Meanwhile, the wiry, redhead had taught him the language of Rhianna's people—Iceni, a necessity when they returned to Britannia. That promise and the images of the woman he loved more than life as well as memories of his son had kept him alive.

Rhianna's pendant of a horse that represented the Iceni tribe shifted across his chest, bringing the ever-present memory of her sliding its chain over his head, whispering, *"As long as you wear this, my soul will be yours."*

"It will never leave me, my love," he whispered. His hand, scarred by vows to Venus, lifted her pendent to his lips as if to seal the promise once again.

Lugh pointed over the railing to the approaching pier where a regal woman searched the galley deck from her cart. "I'm believin' your mother be searchin' for the likes of her son," Lugh said.

Procilla Valeria finally located him on the galley. Her hand lifted to her mouth in shock at seeing her son wearing a filthy tunic, a ragged beard, and shaggy hair spreading across his shoulders. *No, Mother, I am no longer that polished tribune you sent away.*

All of his life, this woman had managed to see that he remained dedicated to Rome and the expectations demanded of all Roman sons: to honor his father's house in all things; to add strength and might to Rome; and to respect the Roman gods that ruled the world. But all of her efforts were now dead to him.

Now, his only focus was to sell the villa and anything else so he could return to Britannia. This time, no one was stopping him. Not Rome. Not his mother. Not his uncle. Not Suetonius. No one.

Yelling broke Julius' attention. The galley's gangplank was now secured to the pier. He rushed to escape what had been his floating prison. The instant his feet found hard surface, he stumbled. Lugh caught his arm. "Dominus?"

He jerked from his slave's touch. He was not a cripple. He could walk. After a few tentative steps, the ground finally steadied beneath him. The crowd parted to retreat from his stench of vomit, filth, and unwashed body. The mere sight of his mother racing toward him turned his insides as cold as the marble statues along the pier. Her radiant smile faded to concern as she reached to enfold him. "Julius, what—!"

He stepped back from her touch. "Mother."

She halted under his unwelcoming snarl, her arms dropping to her sides. "Bona Dea, Julius! You smell worse than the sewer rats in Rome." Straightening, his mother regained her regal composure and covered her nose with a scented cloth. "Why has your slave allowed you to appear like this?" She glared at Lugh.

"Because I no longer care what Rome thinks, Mother." Latin felt foreign—another separation from his old life. Julius smiled. That emotion also seemed foreign.

Quickly scanning anyone close enough to hear his blasphemy, his mother dropped her voice to a warning. "What has come over you Gnaeus Julius Agricola?"

His son's name! Spoken in such a bitter tone cut every nerve in Julius' body. "Nothing, Mother. Absolutely nothing." He started toward the villa that was to give him his freedom.

His mother hurried beside him. "Julius, ride with me. You are in no—

"I will walk."

"Julius. Obviously, you are not strong enough."

"Domina," Lugh cautioned, "I be awarnin' ya this isna the man you left in Britannia. He be a tortured soul, ifn' there ever be one. Had his heart torn out by your brother. Something that shouldna happen to any man."

Snarling at the interruption, his mother turned on Lugh. "How dare you speak to me, slave."

Ignoring their heated argument, Julius passed the long familiar sights that he had wanted to show Rhianna. No place in Britannia could ever have such sun-filled plazas crowded with merchants selling everything she could ever want. Food she had never tasted. Wine she had never drank. Cloth she had never caressed. Aromas she could never imagine. None of it would be enjoyed until Rhianna was by his side again.

Slowly, the noise of the city of Cemenelum evaporated to the peaceful sounds of rustling fields and thick groves of olive trees that stretched over the rolling hillsides bordering the road he walked. Small pebbles of gravel crunched beneath his feet. Fragrant fall breezes swept his path rising gently upward to the distant ridge of the Maritime mountains.

Once, he had loved the essence of everything around him, drank it in like a drunk man. Now, his soul longed for Rhianna's scent of violet flowers, her verdant green hills, Britannia's vibrant weather changes, and its cleansing rains that came unannounced.

Tears blurred his steps as the images of Rhianna floated to him. He longed for her to be walking beside him. Oh, to smell her fragrance and hear her voice or the soft whisper of her sleep beside him again. He wanted to hear the lilting sound of her laughter, the cry of his son. Most of all he wanted the contentment that had consumed them. He let his tears run their course, unhindered.

His mother's mule snorted behind him as her driver drove the cart in the growing afternoon shadows. "Julius. Julius, stop. I have something for you." She climbed from the cart and hurried toward him with a letter. "I . . . I think it best you should read it before we get home."

Made in the USA
Columbia, SC
29 September 2022

68104749R00031